The King's Shopping

JUNE CREBBIN

ILLUSTRATED BY

WARWICK JOHNSON CADWELL

WALKER
BOOKS

For James and all his friends
at Wingfield Nursery
J.C.

For D, H, S and W
W.J.C.

First published 2005 by Walker Books Ltd
87 Vauxhall Walk, London SE11 5HJ

2 4 6 8 10 9 7 5 3 1

Text © 2005 June Crebbin
Illustrations © 2005 Warwick Johnson Cadwell

The right of June Crebbin and Warwick Johnson Cadwell to be identified as
author and illustrator respectively of this work has been asserted by them in
accordance with the Copyright, Designs and Patents Act 1988

This book has been typeset in Bembo Educational

Printed and bound in Great Britain by
Creative Print and Design (Wales), Ebbw Vale

British Library Cataloguing in Publication Data:
a catalogue record for this book
is available from the British Library

ISBN 1-84428-090-X

www.walkerbooks.co.uk

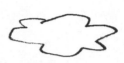

The King's Shopping

The King was in his
counting house,
counting out his money.

He counted out three piles:

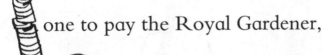 one to pay the Royal Gardener,

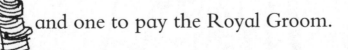 one to pay the Royal Farmer

and one to pay the Royal Groom.

Then he counted what was left. He
wanted to buy something special but he
needed one hundred silver coins.

 "Eighty-eight,  eighty-nine,
 ninety," counted the King…
 "Ninety-eight,  ninety-nine –
 one hundred!"
He leapt into the air.
He had enough! He could
go shopping.

But first he had three important visits to make. No time to lose.

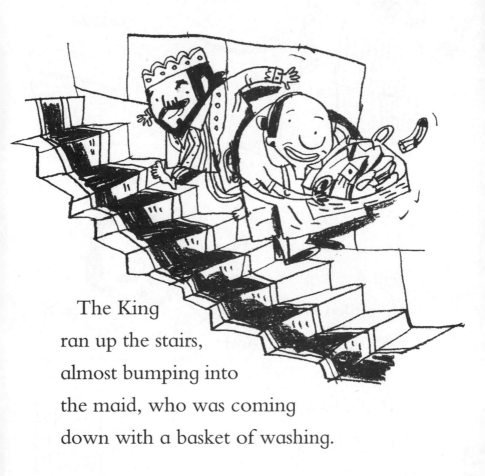

The King
ran up the stairs,
almost bumping into
the maid, who was coming
down with a basket of washing.

He rushed into his room.

He took off his crown, his red dressing gown with the gold braid round the edge and his yellow silk pyjamas.
He pulled on a pair of tracksuit bottoms and a T-shirt.

Then he set off for the kitchen garden.

Ted, the Royal Gardener, was in the greenhouse. The King looked around. Plants of every size and colour filled the shelves. Pots of flowers filled the floor.

"Splendid!" said the King. "Well done!" He handed Ted a bag of coins and quickly turned to leave.

"Thank you!" Ted beamed. "Come and see my tomatoes!"

The King hesitated but Ted was already leading the way.

The King followed. It wouldn't take long.

He admired
the tomatoes and
the kidney beans
and the broad
beans …

… and the rows of
carrots, lettuces, spring onions, peas…

At last the King said
goodbye and set off
for the farm. He
waved to
the Queen
who was
chatting to some children in the
orchard. But he didn't stop. He
couldn't wait to get to the shops.

Dot, the Royal Farmer, was in the
dairy. The King looked around. Jugs,
ladles and milk churns were so clean
they shone.

"Splendid!" said the King. "Well
done!" He handed Dot a bag of coins
and quickly turned to leave.

"Thank you!" Dot beamed. "Come and see my new piglets!"
The King hesitated. But he liked pigs.

The piglets
were pink and
tiny and soft.
The King sat
among them. He
scratched the old
sow behind
her ears.

At last he stood up to
leave. The shops would
soon be closing!

He set off quickly for
the stables.

Ned, the Royal Groom, was in the tack room.

The King looked around. Saddles were stored neatly in rows. Grooming brushes were stored tidily in boxes. Bridles and harnesses were hung on hooks with each horse's name above.

"Splendid!" said the King. "Well done!" He handed Ned a bag of coins and quickly turned to leave.

"Thank you!" Ned beamed. "Come and see Merlin, your new carriage horse. I've just been grooming him."

The King hesitated. But Ned was so proud of the King's horses. It wouldn't take a minute.

Ned brought Merlin out of his stable and trotted him up and down the yard. Merlin's dapple grey coat shone. His silver mane was plaited, showing off the curve of his neck. His silver tail streamed out behind.

20

"Magnificent!" said the King.

He thanked Ned and set off for town.
If he hurried, he could still be there
before the shops shut. But the sun beat
down. It was too hot to walk quickly.

Never mind, the King told himself,
it'll be much more fun on the way back
– and faster!

At last he arrived at
the town and found
the shop he wanted. It was still open.
The King went inside. He'd made it!

Bicycles filled every nook
and cranny. There were
mountain bikes and racing
bikes. There were yellow and
blue and red and
green bikes.

There were bicycles with seats on the back for small children.

There were bicycles with baskets on the front for shopping.

But the King couldn't see the one he wanted.

He explained to the shopkeeper, who
disappeared and came back wheeling a
very special bicycle.

"Splendid!" cried the King.

He handed his one hundred silver
coins to the shopkeeper.
"That's *just* what
I want!"

The Queen's Day Out

The Queen was in the parlour eating bread and honey.

Then she ate a large slice of chocolate cake, three strawberry tartlets and an iced bun.

"Yum, yum!" said the Queen to herself. "I do enjoy a good breakfast."

On her way out to the gardens, she passed a mirror. "Goodness!" she cried. "I'm getting fat. I'd better do some exercise."

The Queen fetched her skipping-rope.

She skipped round and round the rose garden.

She skipped along the path to the kitchen garden, almost bumping into the maid, who was carrying out the clothes.

She skipped up and down between the rows of trees in the orchard.

29

At the edge of the orchard she
came upon some children, weeping.

"Whatever is the matter?" asked
the Queen.

"Our hammock has broken,"
said one.

"A rope has snapped," said another.

"Now we can't swing," said a third.

"I have just the thing!"
cried the Queen.

She tied one end
of her skipping-rope to the end of the
hammock and the other around a tree.

"Try now," she said.

All three children climbed in.

The hammock didn't break. The rope held it.

"Thank you!" said the children.

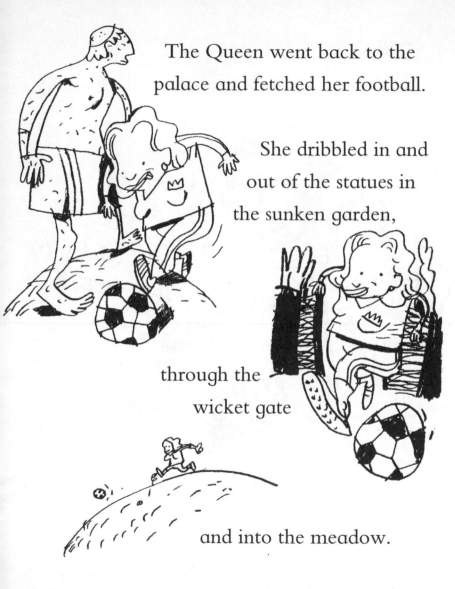

The Queen went back to the palace and fetched her football.

She dribbled in and out of the statues in the sunken garden,

through the wicket gate

and into the meadow.

There she practised some long kicks.

But one kick sent the ball too far.

It landed in the lake.

Ducks flew up in shock.

But by the time the Queen had
brought a long pole from the boathouse
to fish her football out, the ducks had
formed two teams. They were playing
water football!

"Quack! Quack!" they shouted by
way of thanks.

Ah well, thought the Queen. So she
went back to the palace and fetched
her chestnut mare.

She trotted
briskly down the
drive,

out through the iron
gates and up
the road.

After a while she turned
onto the moors and galloped
across the springy heather.

The sun was high. The air was fresh.
The Queen felt fitter by the minute.
Presently she
slowed to a walk.

She came to a
path leading to
a valley, and
down she went.
At the bottom, outside
a cottage, stood a
horse and cart.

A young man
was unloading
vegetables from
the cart.

"Good day!"
said the Queen.

"It may be to you,"
said the young man. "But I cannot take
my vegetables to market because my
horse is lame."

"Borrow mine!" said the Queen. She
jumped off.

"A fine riding horse is no good to
me," complained the young man.

"She also pulls my carriage," said the
Queen.

In no time
at all the chestnut
mare was harnessed to the cart.
The young man thanked the Queen
and set off to market.

The Queen set off back to the palace.

How am I going to keep fit now? she
thought.

Suddenly she heard a noise behind
her, like the tinkling of a bell.
She turned.

It *was* a bell –
a bicycle bell!

"Fancy meeting
you!" cried the King.

"Fancy meeting *you*!" cried the
Queen. "On a bicycle made for two!"

She hopped onto the back of the
King's special bicycle. "This will keep
us both fit!"

And together they
cycled happily
home.

The Maid's Promise

45

The maid was in the garden, hanging out the clothes, when down came a blackbird ...

... but the maid knew his tricks. "Missed me!" she called from behind a frock.
The blackbird was very annoyed.

"Where are you?" he cried, fluttering in and out of the washing. "I only want to play."

"You don't!" said the maid. "You want to peck off my nose. I've heard about you from the last maid."

The blackbird stopped.

At the bottom of the garden the King was admiring tomatoes.

Over in the meadow the Queen was dribbling her football.

The blackbird was thinking. Clearly this maid was going to be more difficult to scare away from his garden than the others.

He thought hard. Then he gave a long whistle.

Charm, he thought. I'll charm the maid, then peck off her nose when she least expects it.

"I'll sing for you," he called. And he threw back his head and sang so loudly, so clearly, so sweetly that the maid was forced to listen.

But as he sang, the maid was thinking.
Sometimes she made a special pie for the
King and Queen – a very dainty dish!
The more she thought, the more she
smiled.

When the blackbird's song came to
an end, the maid came out from
behind the washing.

"That was wonderful," she said.
"You are, without doubt, the finest
singer I have ever heard."

The blackbird's beady eyes glinted.

He hopped towards her.

"In fact," said the maid, "I would say you are the finest singer in the kingdom."

How true, thought the blackbird.

He hopped closer.

HOP

"How would you like to sing for the King and Queen?" asked the maid.

The blackbird trembled. What an honour!

"In the palace?" he asked.

The maid nodded. "At suppertime tonight," she said. "But you must do exactly as I tell you."

"Of course, of course," agreed the blackbird.

After all, he could easily wait until the next day to peck off her nose.

"Come to the window of the palace kitchen at seven o'clock," said the maid.

"I will. See you later!" called the blackbird as he flew away.

The maid picked up the empty washing basket.

But before she went back
inside, she visited all the gardens
in the royal grounds. And in
each garden she spoke to a
number of blackbirds.

That evening, shortly after the King
and Queen had arrived home on their
new bicycle, the blackbird flew down
to the kitchen window. He tapped.

The maid let him in.

"Now," she said, "close your eyes tight."

The blackbird obeyed. The maid carried him across the kitchen. Then he was set down somewhere soft. He wanted to look but, before he knew what was happening, something was drawn over his head and fastened down.

At last he opened his eyes.

He could see nothing. He was trapped!

"Let me out!" he screamed. "Let me out!"

"Only if you promise never to peck off my nose," came the maid's voice.

The blackbird didn't hesitate. "I promise!" he cried.

"They all heard," she said. "All the birds in the pie with you. They heard you promise."

"But *you* promised I could sing for the King and Queen," said the blackbird.

"And so you shall," said the maid.

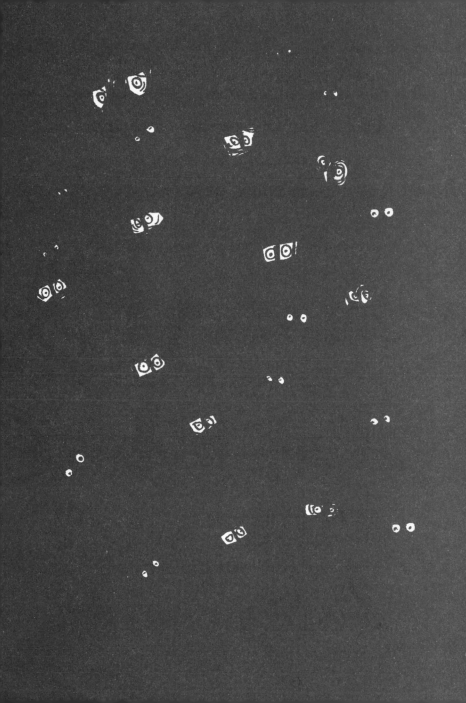

At suppertime, when the pie was opened, four and twenty blackbirds flew out with such a torrent of song that the King and Queen clapped their hands with delight.

And they couldn't help noticing that one blackbird sang more loudly, more clearly and more sweetly than all the rest.